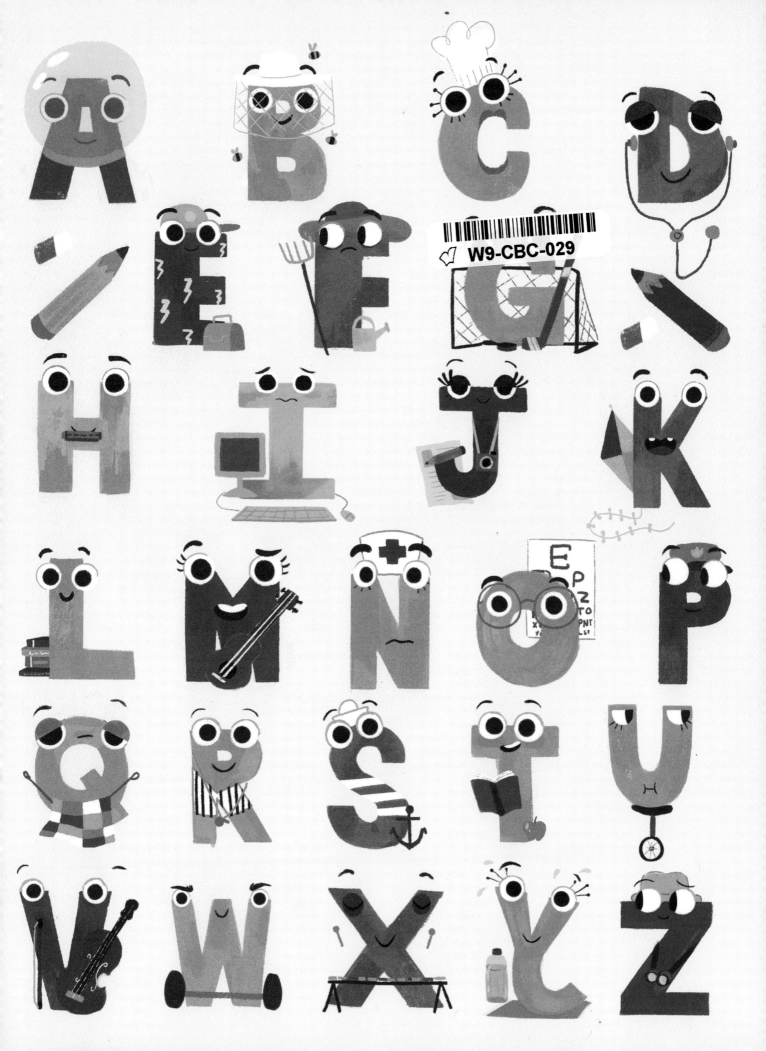

Designed by Flowerpot Press
in Franklin, TN.
www.FlowerpotPress.com
Designer: Stephanie Meyers
Editor: Katrine Crow
DJS-0912-0163
ISBN: 978-1-4867-1211-3
Made in China/Fabriqué en Chine

HOW I Did It!

Written by
Linda Ragsdale

Illustrated by
Anoosha Syed

A B C D E
K L M N O
U V W
X Y Z
F G H J
P Q R S T

In a classroom, surrounded by characters,
I stood straight and tall. I was proud.

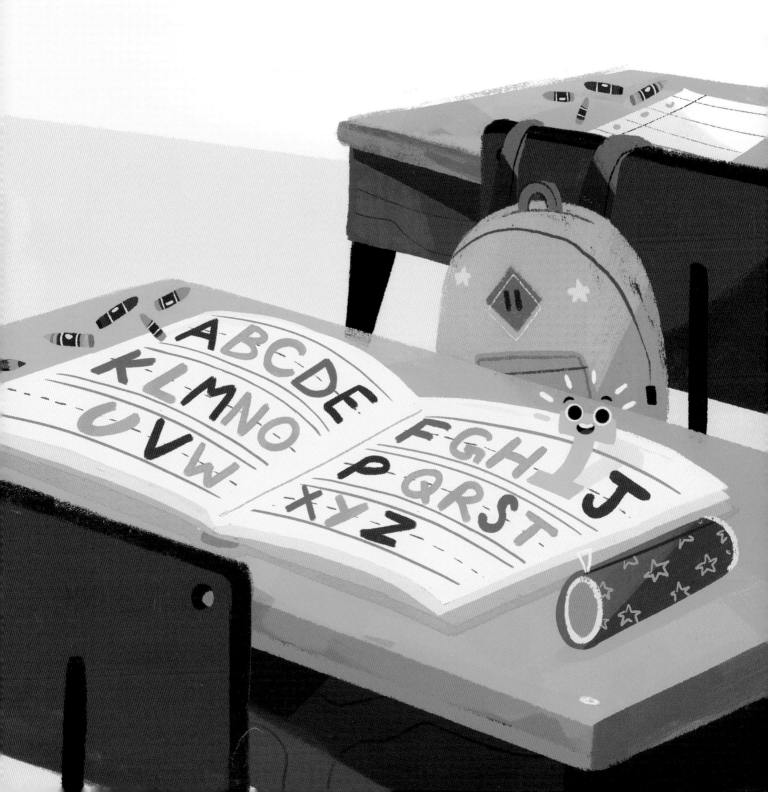

I glanced to the right and thought,
If I turned myself around, I could easily be H.

I was full of ideas.

Then I looked left and saw the most amazing thing!
Oh, I thought, *J is so well-rounded. I could do that.*

So I tried.

"Hey," harrumphed H, "What's happening here?"

"I just want to try to curve like J," I said.

"Hah," harped H.

Why, if you get all bent out of shape, you'll be erased for sure! Quit being a joker!

Joker?!

"I can change if I choose.
I'm not written in ink!"

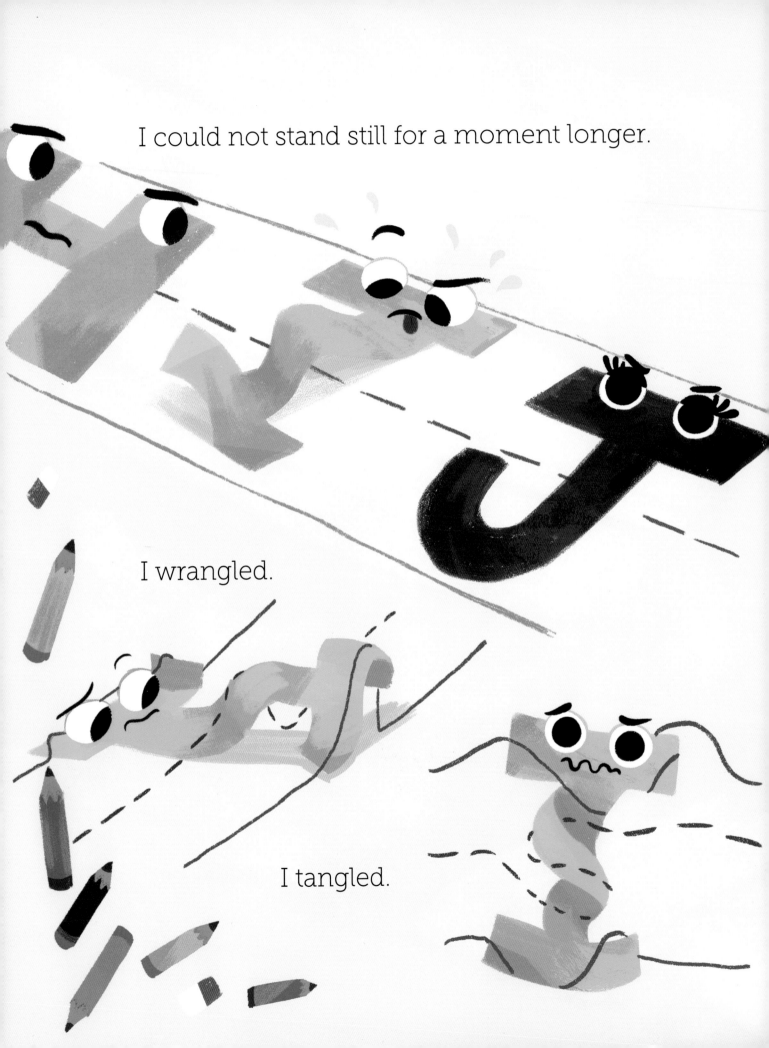

I yanked on the lines and... POP!

WOO-HOO!

A B C D E
K L M N O
U V W
F G H J
P Q R S T
X Y Z

I broke free with a loud exclamation!

Wriggling like an inchworm,
I scrinched and scrunched between the lines.

I had a whole new point of view.

E yelled,

"TAKE it EASY!"

F frowned over the fuss.

"Good Grief!"

gasped G.

"Ooooh," said O.
"Outstanding!"

T was tickled.

What's wrong with wandering?

wondered W.

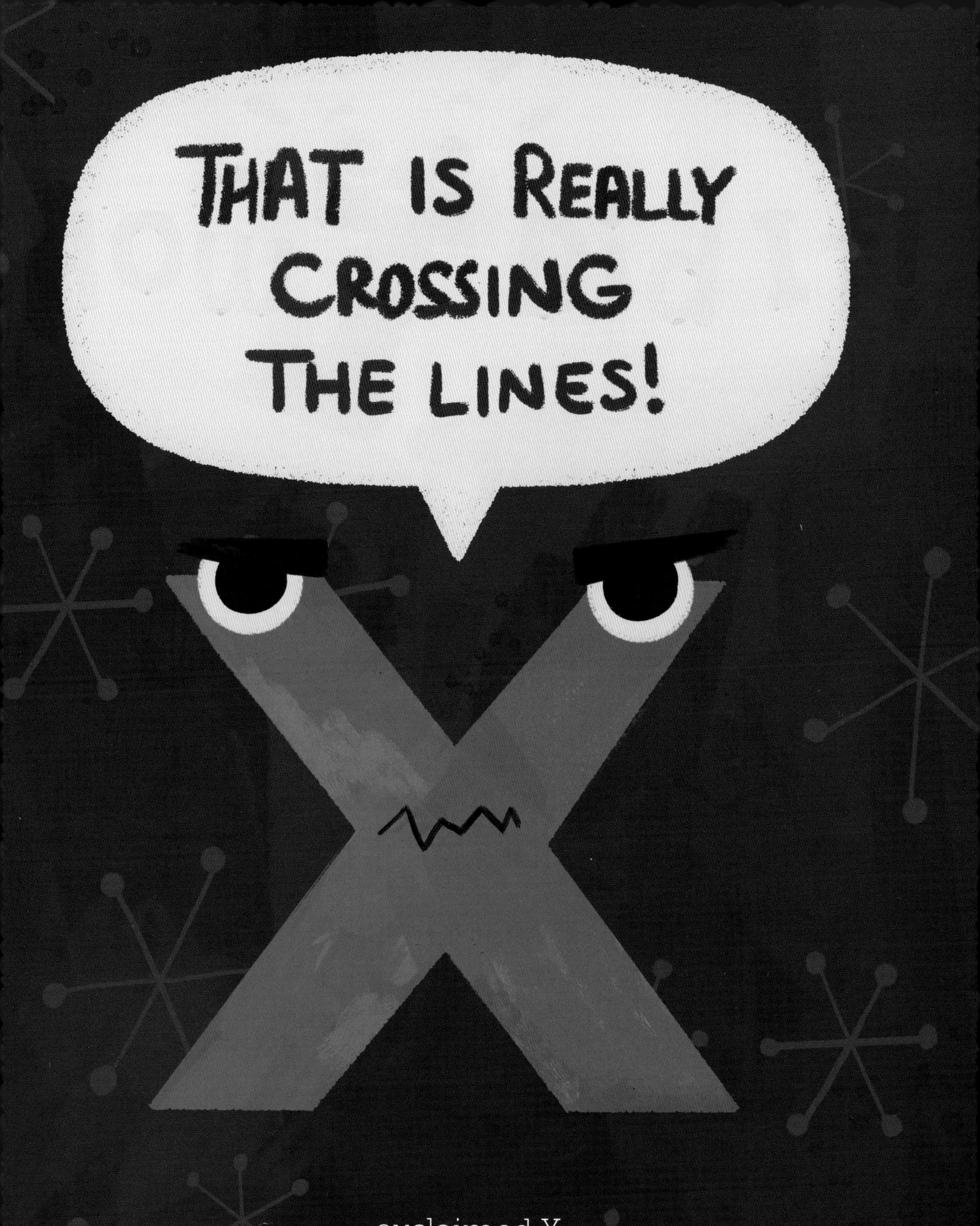

exclaimed X.

As I reached for new heights,
A saw what C saw,
and they could not believe what I was doing!

B just let it be.

I ignored them all. I kept going.

In the middle of a scrunch, I stood up.

I began to walk, then run.

I leapt, skipped, and danced along the dotted lines.

I was really on the move!

But I was too excited to notice...

I didn't see it coming.
The trouble ahead.
The end of the line.

That's when I fell.

I was a mess. Crumpled and twisted.

I felt like nothing more than a scribble.

I didn't move. I couldn't move.

I didn't know where I started or ended.

"You should have minded your p's and q's and stayed in the lines," pompously quipped P and Q.

"So sad..." sighed S.

S was right. I *was* so sad.

I curled up into a ball. I wasn't going to take any
more chances. I was done. This was it. Period.

Or was I? I took a good look.
I realized...I *was* well-rounded!

I was not done.

I had so much more to do.

I had so many more things to try.

If I focused on flipping, I flipped.

If I wanted, I could curl, swirl, twist, and turn.

I could do anything. I could be anything.
Anything I wanted to be.
Anything all the way from A to Z.
I was full of possibilities!

twist!

turn

I was ready to explore them all.
I knew I could do it!

Just as I was about to head off on a new adventure,
I looked up and I saw U.
And I knew...

U could do it too.